Paisley Atoms

SPACING OUT

By Kyla Steinkraus

Illustrated by Alan Brown

Rourke
Educational Media
rourkeeducationalmedia.com

www.rourkeeducationalmedia.com

Edited by: Keli Sipperley
Cover and Interior layout by: Rhea Magaro-Wallace
Cover and Interior Illustrations by: Alan Brown

Library of Congress PCN Data

Spacing Out / Kyla Steinkraus
(Paisley Atoms)
ISBN (hard cover)(alk. paper) 978-1-68191-711-5
ISBN (soft cover) 978-1-68191-812-9
ISBN (e-Book) 978-1-68191-907-2
Library of Congress Control Number: 2016932588

Printed in the United States of America,
North Mankato, Minnesota

Dear Parents and Teachers,

Future world-famous scientist Paisley Atoms and her best friend, Ben Striker, aren't afraid to stir things up in their quests for discovery. Using Paisley's basement as a laboratory, the two are constantly inventing, exploring, and, well, making messes. Paisley has a few bruises to show for their work, too. She wears them like badges of honor.

These fast-paced adventures weave fascinating facts, quotes from real scientists, and explanations for various phenomena into witty dialogue, stealthily boosting your reader's understanding of multiple science topics. From sound waves to dinosaurs, from the sea floor to the moon, Paisley, Ben and the gang are perfect partner resources for a STEAM curriculum.

Each illustrated chapter book includes a science experiment or activity, a biography of a woman in science, jokes, and websites to visit.

In addition, each book also includes online teacher/parent notes with ideas for incorporating the story into a lesson plan. These notes include subject matter, background information, inspiration for maker space activities, comprehension questions, and additional online resources. Notes are available at: www.RourkeEducationalMedia.com.

We hope you enjoy Paisley and her pals as much as we do.

Happy reading,
Rourke Educational Media

TABLE OF CONTENTS

CHAPTER ONE
EPIC ARGUMENTS

Paisley Atoms bounced in her seat. She looked forward to science with Mrs. Beaker every single day. Paisley loved science more than almost anything. Except her parents, of course. And her pet mongoose, Newton. And her best friend, Ben Striker.

"Good morning, class," said Mrs. Beaker, the fifth-grade science teacher. She stood in the front of the classroom and stretched out her hands. "It is time for our moment of science." Mrs. Beaker started every class with that pun. The class had to be absolutely quiet for thirty seconds. It was much harder than it sounded. The class had learned not to groan or the moment of silence would be extended indefinitely.

Paisley put her hands on her desk and stared straight ahead. If she looked at Ben on the right or her friend Arjun on the left, one of them would make a face and start them all giggling.

Mrs. Beaker smiled broadly. "Fantastic. Now, everyone please turn to chapter seven in your textbooks. We are starting our unit on outer space. Thousands of years ago, the world thought that Earth was the center of the universe."

"Whitney-Raelynn thinks she's the center of the universe," Arjun said. Several students snickered.

"I heard that!" Whitney-Raelynn snapped. She smoothed her perfectly straight and glossy blonde hair with her fingers. "Isn't it true?"

Even though she sounded like she was joking, everyone knew she really wasn't. Whitney-Raelynn thought she was God's gift to Roarington Elementary. Unfortunately, she was actually pretty smart and super talented at anything she tried. It was extremely irritating.

"Anyhoo," Mrs. Beaker said, ignoring the class. "Now we know that our solar system revolves around the sun."

Paisley's hand shot up. "The astronomer Nicolaus Copernicus discovered that in 1543."

"Ah, yes, Paisley, that is correct. Thank you for that contribution," Mrs. Beaker said. "Our galaxy is known as the Milky Way. Our solar system is inside the Milky Way. It is made up of all of the planets that orbit the sun, along with stars, moons, comets, asteroids, smaller minor planets—"

"Go Pluto!" Rosalind yelled. Rosalind was the class clown.

"Yes. As we all know, Pluto is now considered a dwarf planet. There are eight actual planets. Who would like to name them?"

Paisley's hand shot up again, but Mrs. Beaker called on Ben. Everyone knew Ben loved astronomy. His parents had named him after the astronomer and mathematician Benjamin Banneker. Ben also loved clocks, inventing things, and the creepy, crawly creatures in the ant colonies and worm farms he kept in his closet instead of clothes. Paisley and Ben were not only best friends, they'd been next-door neighbors since they were both in diapers. Ben cleared his throat. "Starting from the sun: Mercury, Venus, Earth, Mars, Jupiter, Saturn, Uranus, and Neptune. Would you like their sizes and distances from Earth?"

"Not right now. Although, I'm sure you know them by heart. Thank you, Ben. We will start with the gas giants."

"Arjun is a gas giant!" said a boy named Colton. Several boys behind Paisley snickered.

Paisley rolled her eyes. "The gas giants are the four farthest planets from the sun. They are made of a swirling mix of gases like hydrogen and helium, with a liquid metal or rock core."

"And Uranus and Neptune are made up of ammonia and methane," Ben added. "Methane is what gives them their blue color."

"Yes, that's right, once again," Mrs. Beaker said with a sigh. She always seemed a bit disappointed when Paisley and Ben knew all the answers already. "Let's begin with Jupiter, shall we?"

"Are there aliens on Jupiter?" Rosalind asked.

"Raise your hand, please," Mrs. Beaker said.

Rosalind raised her hand. "Are there aliens on Jupiter?"

"Well, we don't really know," Mrs. Beaker said.

"But isn't it possible?" Sumi asked. Sumi had straight black hair to her chin and brown eyes that always sparkled with mischief. She and her identical twin, Suki, pulled pranks, told jokes, and switched places whenever possible. Paisley was the only person who could tell them apart every time.

"Well, I don't know, Suki. I suppose it's possible."

Sumi smiled sweetly and winked at Paisley.

"Why did the alien spit out the clown?" Rosalind asked. She paused for effect. "Because he tasted funny!"

"Ha ha. Good joke," Whitney-Raelynn said. "But aliens couldn't live on Jupiter. There's nothing but gas to walk on."

Colton snickered again.

"But aliens on Jupiter could have less mass," Paisley said. "They could be so light, they float. They could breathe helium or hydrogen instead of oxygen."

"Don't be so dork-tastic, Atoms," Whitney-Raelynn countered. "Jupiter is like negative two hundred and ninety degrees. The whole planet is a massive storm. Life forms need water and oxygen, neither of which are on that planet. There are no life forms on Jupiter."

"But the life forms could have a totally different design than human beings," Paisley said. "It's so narrow-minded to think they would have to breathe the same stuff we do."

Whitney-Raelynn crossed her arms. "Looks like I overestimated your brain cell count. Astrobiologists have found zero signs of life on any of the planets in our solar system. Like, not even microorganisms like bacteria and plankton."

"I agree," Ben said.

Paisley looked at him sharply. "What?"

"Believe it or not, I agree with Whitney-Raelynn. There are no silly little green men on Jupiter or any other planet."

Whitney-Raelynn grinned in triumph. Ugh. Paisley couldn't stand even looking at her.

She glared at Ben instead. What was he thinking? One never agreed with Whitney-Raelynn, even when she was right! And in this case, she most certainly was not. "It is not silly! They wouldn't be little green men, obviously. That's just from the movies. Just because we need oxygen doesn't mean an alien would. Such a being would have adapted to their specific planet's environment in ways we don't understand yet."

Mrs. Beaker cleared her throat. "Great discussion, guys. Let's bring this back to—"

"How could aliens survive without oxygen?" Whitney-Raelynn asked, raising one perfectly arched eyebrow. "NASA has been studying space for decades, and they haven't found anything. Enough said."

"Not that you'll understand this, being as you're from the shallow end of the gene pool yourself," Paisley said. "But scientists have found multicellular organisms deep beneath the Mediterranean Sea that are anaerobic; they don't have mitochondria, and they don't metabolize oxygen. One is called Spinoloricus." Paisley remembered the article her father had shown her. Dad was a biologist and professor for the state university thirty minutes outside of Roarington–also known as Boring Town, USA.

"That's a bunch of science fiction. Never trust Atoms. They make up everything," Whitney-Raelynn said, using her favorite insult for Paisley. She thought it was hilarious, since all matter is made up of atoms. Paisley did not find it hilarious.

"I can explain it to you but I can't understand it for you," Paisley snapped.

"Paisley is right, about the anaerobic organisms at least," Ben conceded. "But it doesn't mean anything. Unless your idea of an alien is a microscopic, squid-like creature that's less than a millimeter long."

Paisley scowled at him. Traitor. "Of course not. I—"

Mrs. Beaker clapped her hands. "What a great topic for a homework assignment. Let's save our enthusiasm for a one-page paper on whether we think aliens exist, and why or why not."

The class groaned.

"You're welcome," Whitney-Raelynn said smugly.

"What should you do if you see an alien?" Rosalind asked, then answered her own question: "Hope he doesn't see you!"

"Lovely joke, Rosalind," Mrs. Beaker said. She sounded tired. "Now, class, let's focus on our textbook, shall we?"

Normally Paisley would offer comments and suggestions throughout class, much to Mrs. Beaker's exasperation. But today she slumped in her seat, barely able to listen to Mrs. Beaker explain the basic properties of each of the planets. Whitney-Raelynn's usual arguments didn't faze her. But Ben taking Whitney-Raelynn's side against Paisley? That was all kinds of wrong.

CHAPTER TWO
OUT OF THIS WORLD

Paisley's whole mood soured. When she walked home from school, she didn't stop to talk to her neighbor, six-year-old Mia Pendlebury, who was collecting a pile of rocks and sticks on her front porch. The front of her ruffled pink lace dress was smeared with dirt. Her mother, the fastidious Mrs. Pendlebury, would definitely not approve.

"Hiya!" Mia called. Mia's pudgy cheeks were framed by chocolate brown ringlets. She always wanted to know what inventions Paisley was working on in her basement lab. "Whatcha doing? Wanna come see my worm garden?"

Paisley just yanked on her backpack straps and kept walking. "Sorry, not right now, kiddo."

Mia's face fell. "Okay."

Paisley felt a stab of remorse. But she kept walking. Her head felt like one big angry thundercloud. She hadn't even walked home with Ben; she was that mad.

She stomped into the house and dropped her backpack on the floor.

Paisley's pet Indian gray mongoose Newton slid down the staircase bannister and leaped onto Paisley's shoulder. He chirped and stuck his wet nose into her ear, his version of saying hello. She rubbed his soft gray fur. Mom had brought him home from one of her research trips to India.

"Bad day, honey?" Dad asked from behind his computer. Dozens of papers were scattered across the kitchen table. He was working on a big research project on microscopic organisms for the university.

"Sort of," she answered. "How's your work?"

Dad removed his black-rimmed glasses and rubbed his eyes. "Science is a wonderful thing if one does not have to earn one's living at it," he said, quoting Albert Einstein. "And a lot more fun, too."

"That good, huh?" Paisley moved a pile of papers from a chair and sat down next to Dad.

Dad patted her shoulder. "You're the one who looks like you just lost the science fair. Tell me about it."

Paisley told him about the science class discussion. "I can't believe Ben betrayed me."

"Others are entitled to their own opinions, you know," Dad said gently.

"Yeah but with HER? Ugh." Paisley buried her face in her hands. "Besides, I'm right. I know it."

"Just remember, 'The scientist is not a person who gives the right answers, he's one who asks the right questions,'" Dad said, quoting one of his favorite scientists, Claude Levi-Strauss. "It's not about being right all the time."

Paisley just sighed.

"Why don't you Skype Mom? She's much better at this kind of thing." Mom was a botanist. She was on a research project in Mexico, trying to find the thought-to-be-extinct chocolate cosmos growing in the wild. The chocolate cosmos was a beautiful burgundy flower that smelled like chocolate.

"Oh, all right," Paisley said. A conversation with

Mom did sound good. She fingered the ancient key she wore on a chain around her neck, a gift from Mom when she turned five. The key contained a special energy that Paisley used to go on grand adventures and power up some of her and Ben's inventions. Mom sure knew how to give awesome gifts.

Before she could get on the computer, there was a knock on the door.

It was Ben. He stood on the front porch, holding his field journal notebook to his chest. Paisley stared at him. "What do you want?"

Ben usually came over every day after school. They fiddled around in Paisley's basement laboratory inventing things, conducting experiments, and occasionally blowing stuff up, just like Thomas Edison did in his own basement laboratory when he was a boy. After experimenting, Ben would have supper with Paisley and Dad. Then he would go home for "second supper" with his own parents, who were both engineers and worked long hours.

"I know we disagreed today," Ben said mildly.

"That's an understatement," Paisley muttered.

"But I don't want disagreements to affect our friendship, okay? You're really important to me."

Sometimes it was really hard to stay mad at Ben. "Okay, fine."

"Besides, I have an idea. Let's settle this debate our way."

Paisley's face brightened. She liked where this was going. "You mean . . ."

"Yes!" Ben showed her a page in his field journal. He'd drawn some type of ship with arrows and diagrams and labeled parts.

"Is that what I think it is?" Paisley asked, her blood thumping in excitement.

"A rocket ship! Let's visit our solar system and see for ourselves whether there's life on other planets."

Paisley shrugged, but she was grinning from ear to ear. "Sure. Why not? I've got nothing else to do this afternoon."

CHAPTER THREE
IT'S NOT ROCKET SCIENCE

Paisley and Ben hurried down to Paisley's basement lab. "Hi, Mr. Atoms!" Ben called.

"Hiya, Ben! Have fun, you two," Paisley's dad said. He frowned at his computer. "More fun than I'll have, I bet."

Paisley's lab was stuffed full of junk. The best junk on the planet, Paisley thought. She had a table full of beakers, tubes, slides, and an old microscope. Shelves against one wall held buckets of nails, nuts and bolts, water bottles, soda cans, flashlights, light bulbs, rubber bands, batteries, safety pins, a spatula, PVC pipe, copper wire, hand mirrors, and knee pads. She'd picked up various discarded belongings from neighbors and Mr. Wreck's Junkyard, which were now shoved into every available corner: a metal trash can, an old surfboard, bicycle wheels, two umbrellas, a broken tennis racket, a fishing pole, a pair of skis, and a crate on roller skates. She also had a toolbox with pliers, a hacksaw, a screw gun, and of course, safety goggles. The toxic chemicals were locked in a cupboard with CAUTION: DANGEROUS scrawled across the front in permanent marker.

"I have a bunch of ideas already," Paisley said excitedly as she yanked her wavy hair back into its usual messy bun. "A rocket uses massive amounts of liquid hydrogen and liquid oxygen that gets mixed at lift-off. As the fuel burns in the combustion chamber, it creates a blast of exhaust gas, producing an equal force reaction that propels the rocket upward into space. I don't think Dad would let us set off an explosion as big as we'd need in the backyard, so we need to try something else."

"We must reach an escape velocity of at least twenty-five thousand miles per hour to escape Earth's gravity," Ben said, gazing at his field book.

Paisley picked up a bottle of vinegar and stared at it. "I have an idea for fuel. I've got baking soda and vinegar. We'll mix them together in an air-tight container. The chemical reaction creates carbon dioxide gases, which will cause a rapid increase in pressure. The force of the reaction should propel us into space, with a little help, of course," she said, fingering the ancient key around her neck.

"The dream of today is the reality of tomorrow," Ben said, paraphrasing a quote from Robert Hutchings Goddard, the father of rocketry.

"No, the dream of today is the reality of today. Let's do this!" They wrote down a list of supplies. Paisley grabbed her old Radio Flyer wagon from the garage. Her parents never could get rid of stuff. They borrowed two cushions from the couch in the living room for seats.

"I expect those back!" Dad yelled from the kitchen.

Paisley lugged in a large canister with knobs to release the gas. They attached it to the back of the wagon with a bundle of super stretchy bungee cord. "We'll put the fuel in here, so we can control how much is released."

Next, Ben dismantled the handlebars from Paisley's bike to use for steering. They cut wing shapes out of a large piece of plywood and superglued them to the sides of the Radio Flyer. Ben attached a thermometer.

"Don't forget, we need to re-enter Earth's atmosphere

on the return trip," Paisley said. We'll be traveling thousands of miles an hour and creating crazy amounts of kinetic energy. We need a heat retardant."

They painted everything with a layer of glue and pressed sheets of aluminum foil over every inch of the spaceship. "How reflective," Ben said.

"We need to protect ourselves, too. It'll be cold in space." Paisley retrieved two winter coats from the coat closet.

"What is this?" Ben asked, holding up a puffy purple coat with pink flowers all over it.

"My dad's coat is too big for you. And you certainly can't have mine. Mom's fits you just right."

Ben groaned. "Fine."

"No one will see you in it, I promise," Paisley said, handing him Mom's pair of sparkly pink gloves. "You're welcome."

Paisley stared at the spaceship. There was still something missing . . . "Aha! We need space helmets! And I know just where to get them!" She pointed up at the basement window, where six-year-old Mia was peering in at them.

Paisley ran up the stairs and out to the side yard. "Mia? Can you help us? Can we borrow your fish bowls?"

Mia nodded, her eyes huge. "Are you going into outer space?"

Paisley put her finger to her lips. "Our secret, okay?"

Mia led Paisley through her fancy, neat-as-a-pin home. Mia's bedroom looked like it was out of a magazine. Mia pointed to two beautiful blue fish with long, fan-like fins, each swimming in their own large glass bowl. "This is Bacon and this is Eggs. They're Siamese Fighting Fish. Where will they swim without their fish bowls?"

"Where's your bathtub?" Paisley asked. She and Mia filled a bathtub with warm water.

Mia giggled as she dumped Bacon and then Eggs into the bathtub. "They'll have a vacation!"

Paisley promised to bring the fish bowls back after supper. She raced back to the lab. They dragged the spacecraft up the stairs and out to the backyard. She sat on the front cushion, and Ben clambered into the back. Paisley adjusted her fish bowl helmet. "It's our very own Space Flyer!"

"Let's hope it works," Ben said. "I have a bad feeling about this."

"You have a bad feeling about everything. It'll work." She grabbed the ancient key and held it against the Space Flyer. "Please work," she whispered.

She and Ben grinned at each other as they fist bumped. "Science Alliance!"

The Space Flyer shook and roared. Paisley's teeth rattled in her head. One second they were in Paisley's backyard, the next second they were hurtling into the sky. They shot up so fast Paisley barely glimpsed the trees, houses, and cars a dizzying distance below. She closed her eyes as the air sizzled and burned in front of them as they passed through Earth's atmosphere. There were some things it was better not to see.

She tried to speak, but the roaring whooshing in her ears was so loud she could barely hear herself think. She, Paisley Atoms, future scientific genius and discoverer of life on other planets, was on her way to outer space!

CHAPTER FOUR
SEARCHING FOR ALIENS

Paisley opened her eyes. They were surrounded by space. It was absolutely silent. There was no breeze. No horns honking. No birds chirping. Nothing. Bright stars were everywhere. They shone brilliant and colorful; some were blue, some were green, red, and yellow. "Do you see this?" she said to Ben.

Ben looked at her. His eyes were huge behind his glasses. He grinned a big, goofy grin. "This is awesome!"

Paisley pointed at something behind Ben. "What is that big white thing?" It was large and round like a cue ball, and very far away.

"That's the sun," Ben said. "It only seems yellow to us on Earth because of our atmosphere."

"Of course," Paisley said. "The sun is a star."

Ahead of them, a massive planet loomed. It was tan and banded with streaks of white and rust. Up close, she could see the swirling gases of helium and hydrogen. "Jupiter!" Paisley said in awe.

"More than thirteen hundred Earths can fit inside Jupiter," Ben said.

"I believe it."

"There's nowhere to land, Paisley. We'd sink straight through to the rocky core, where we'd be crushed by millions of pounds of gas. I don't want to win the bet that badly. Let's look for a moon. Jupiter has sixty-four of them."

Paisley gasped. "Look! That's Europa, one of the Galilean moons! Galileo discovered that moon in 1610!"

Ben adjusted the direction of the jet fuel and Paisley steered the Space Flyer. They rocketed down to the surface of Europa. Ben and Paisley slammed forward as the wagon made a rough landing.

Paisley rubbed her head. "Ouch!" She climbed out

and looked around. Jupiter was a massive disc blotting out half the sky. The whole surface of Europa was crusted with ice. Ridges and cracks crisscrossed the ice wherever they looked. To their right was a massive canyon.

Paisley took a step and sailed a few feet before landing. "Gravity here is one-sixth what it is on Earth. I can jump eight feet in the air! Look!" She took several long, floating leaps to the canyon's edge. "These are caused by Jupiter's strong gravitational pull," Paisley said, peering over the edge.

Ben grabbed her arm. "Careful!"

"I'm looking for extraterrestrial life! Researchers think life could exist in the oceans beneath this mantle of ice."

"That's possible, but diving into a planetary canyon isn't going to help you find your little green aliens. There's no way to get down there and prove it."

"How convenient for you." Paisley stuck her tongue out at him as she adjusted her helmet. "Doesn't this atmosphere contain oxygen?"

"Yes, but it's much too thin for us to actually breathe."

"But a different life form could," Paisley said. She rubbed her arms. The bitter cold was beginning to seep through her protective clothing. "This is wayyyy too cold."

"It's negative two hundred sixty degrees."

"Exactly. Let's get outta here!" Paisley said between chattering teeth.

Next, they headed for Saturn, another gas giant. "I always loved Saturn's rings," Paisley sighed as they zoomed close to the beautiful yellowish planet. They could see huge chunks of ice and rock whirling around Saturn in swirling rings. Galileo had discovered Saturn's rings, too.

"We can't land here, either," Ben said. "Saturn's winds can reach up to eleven hundred miles an hour. That's four times stronger than any hurricane ever recorded on Earth."

Paisley pointed. "Land on that moon. It's called Titan. It's the largest moon in the solar system." They flew the Space Flyer down to the surface of the moon. This landing was a bit smoother.

"It's freezing here, too," Ben said, shivering. "I guess minus two hundred ninety degrees is really cold."

Paisley laughed. "If we lived here, we wouldn't need a pressurized suit to survive. All we'd need is an oxygen mask and warm clothes."

"Very warm clothes!"

Titan's sky was a smoggy orange and filled with dense clouds. Saturn filled a third of the sky. The surface of the moon was mostly flat, covered with ice rocks and small dunes. Several large lakes shimmered in the distance. "Those lakes are filled with liquid methane," Paisley said. "Life forms could subsist on methane the same way we need water."

Paisley felt almost as light as air. She skipped up a nearby dune. "Come try!" she called to Ben.

Ben shook his head. "Whatever you're about to do, I'm pretty sure I do not want to do it."

"Your loss!" she said as she unzipped her coat. She ignored the blast of icy air. Spreading her coat on either side of her body, she leapt off the dune and glided down to Ben. "It's almost like flying!"

Ben nodded. "It must be because of Titan's dense atmosphere. And because it's gravity is only twelve percent of Earth's, you only weigh around twelve pounds here. The air is thick, almost like water. Instead of swimming, you can glide."

"It's awesome! Hey, look at the sun!" The sun was a distant, golf ball-sized shape in the orange sky. Paisley shook her hands. She couldn't feel her fingers! "Speaking of the sun, can we head a bit closer to it, for some warmth?"

"We could visit Venus, but I am quite sure there is no life there," Ben said firmly.

"Yeah, it would be hard for any life in eight hundred seventy degree temperatures. That's twice as hot as an oven!"

Ben checked the fuel gauge. "We're getting low on rocket fuel. Remember, we've got to get home, too."

"Okay, just one more?" Paisley asked.

"Well, in theory, I suppose—"

"Excellent! Let's go to Mars!"

CHAPTER FIVE
PHOTOGENIC MARTIANS

Soon the fourth planet from the sun loomed in front of them. The planet had a reddish hue from all the iron oxide on its surface. Even though Mars was half the diameter of Earth, up close it still looked huge.

Paisley landed the Space Flyer with barely a bump. "It's downright balmy here!" she said, stretching out her arms. "We must be near the equator. It's almost sixty degrees."

"Don't take off your protective gear," Ben warned. "Unlike Earth, Mars doesn't have a magnetic field and thick atmosphere to protect the surface from radiation."

The sky had a slight orange tint from all the dust. In the distance, Paisley could see mountain ranges, deep valleys, long ridges, canyons, and massive stretches of desert.

"It's all just red rock and sand," Paisley said, kicking at the ground in frustration.

Ben patted her shoulder. "They did find evidence water once existed here. They could find more."

"I guess." Paisley sighed. She hated losing. She knew there was life somewhere in this solar system, but she couldn't prove it.

"I'd love to visit Olympus Mons," Ben said wistfully. "It is the tallest mountain in the solar system. It's sixteen miles high, three times taller than Mount Everest."

"Next time," Paisley said.

Suddenly, something moved in the distance. Paisley's heart leaped in her chest. Could she have just discovered extraterrestrial life? Images of herself receiving awards and accolades flashed through her mind. Maybe she'd even get to name the alien! She grabbed the binoculars from the Space Flyer and focused the lens. "Wait—what?"

"It's the Opportunity Rover!" Ben said. "It's been

exploring Mars and taking pictures to send back to NASA since 2003!"

Paisley felt a pang of disappointment in her gut. Discovering the solar system's first alien would have been totally cool. Still, the rover was pretty cool, too. It had a long neck with a camera at the top, a body fitted with solar panels for energy, antennae, a mechanical arm, and four wheels to transport it over the rocky terrain of Mars. The neck turned toward them. "Do you think it's taking a picture of us? Will NASA think we're aliens?"

"I hope not," Ben said. "I'll never hear the end of it: 'Famous Space Boy in Flowered Coat!'"

Paisley giggled.

"Uh oh."

"What?"

"I think we might have bigger problems!" Ben said.

Paisley lowered the binoculars. She gasped. At first glance, what looked like a range of mountains quickly transformed into a massive wave; a wave that appeared to be rolling closer. A huge dust storm thundered toward them.

"We've got to get out of here!" Paisley yelled over the growing roar. Dust swirled all around them. The wind whipped at her clothing, almost knocking her over.

"We're almost out of fuel!" Ben yelled back.

"We've got to go! Aim for Earth!"

Rising plumes of sand blasted them as they leaped into the Space Flyer. They flew up, up, up, rocketing up out of Mars's atmosphere and into space. Paisley wiped a film of dust off of her fishbowl helmet. "Ugh, this stuff is everywhere."

"Those dust storms can last for weeks," Ben said. "Once every several years, there's a storm so big it covers the entire planet!"

"It's much more interesting to talk about than to experience," Paisley said, wiping off her suit and the Space Flyer.

"Paisley! Watch out!" Ben shouted. "You're headed straight for that asteroid!"

Paisley yanked on the Space Flyer handlebars, but they barely moved. Mars sand was caked inside the

mechanism, making the handlebars difficult to turn. The huge rock filled their vision. "Turn! Turn!" Paisley screamed at the Space Flyer.

The handlebars squealed and budged slightly. Ben released a tiny burst of fuel. They jetted forward at a forty-five-degree angle. The massive shadow of the asteroid slid over them. "We're not gonna make it!" Ben cried.

Adrenaline pumped through Paisley's veins. She felt cold and dizzy as she wrenched the handlebars with all her might. The Space Flyer scraped the side of the asteroid with a terrible groaning, screeching sound. One of the couch cushions ripped, and ribbons of stuffing floated into space.

And then they were free!

"I told you we'd make it," Ben said in a squeaky voice.

"That was too close for comfort," Paisley said.

They coasted for a few minutes in silence. "I see Earth!" Ben said.

It was the most beautiful planet Paisley had ever seen. Even though she hadn't won the bet, she was ready to go home. "Ben, are you sure we're on the correct trajectory?"

Ben fiddled with his instruments. "Um. Well, unfortunately it appears that the asteroid knocked us off course."

"Get us back on course!"

"Ah. Um. It appears we can't. We are also out of fuel."

CHAPTER SIX
A DISASTER OF
MINOR PROPORTIONS

Paisley took several deep, calming breaths. It didn't make her feel calm. "Can we reach the moon, at least?"

Ben did several calculations in his head. "Yes."

"Okay. We'll figure it out from there."

The Space Flyer shot through space. The moon loomed larger and larger. Paisley tried to land softly. But without the handlebars for steering, the wagon hit nose first. Ben and Paisley tumbled out. It felt like colliding with an elephant.

Paisley groaned and rubbed her neck. "I hit my head so hard, I'm seeing stars! A whole galaxy!"

Ben laughed.

Her knees ached. "At least I'll have some cool bruises."

"I'm going to be sore for days," Ben said. "Weeks."

The moon's surface was gray and bleak. In the distance, Paisley could see massive craters and even mountains. Rocks of various sizes jutted out from the gravelly soil. She took a couple of floating steps and sat down on a large stone. "It's really hot here," she said. She was already sweating inside her thick coat. Paisley remembered Mrs. Beaker's talk earlier that day. The moon's temperature averaged two hundred and fifty-two degrees during the day.

Ben sat next to her. "Just wait until it gets dark. Then it'll be a freezing minus two hundred ninety-eight degrees."

"That actually sounds refreshing right now."

Ben's stomach rumbled. "If I'd known lunch was going to be my last meal, I would've had thirds."

Paisley laughed. "Don't be a lunatic! We'll get home somehow. Get it, luna-tic?"

"Yeah," Ben said, unconvinced.

Paisley elbowed him. "Think like a proton and stay positive."

This time Ben smiled. "I'm trying."

Suddenly Paisley gasped. "Look. Earth."

Straight in front of them, as if hung from the ceiling of the universe, a light blue sphere laced with swirls of soft white shimmered against the blackness of space. It was perfectly round and as brightly colored as a jewel. It was the most beautiful thing Paisley had ever seen.

For a long moment neither of them spoke. Paisley felt very, very small. Just a speck in the universe. Her epic argument with Ben and Whitney-Raelynn didn't seem very epic anymore. "I'm sorry," she said finally. "It's okay to disagree and have different opinions. I overreacted."

"I forgive you," Ben said. They exchanged grins.

"It looks close enough to touch, doesn't it?" Paisley asked. She blinked away the sweat dripping down her face. She felt cooked. Baked. Roasted.

"It's not. All the planets in our solar system can fit between the moon and Earth," Ben said. "We're still far from home."

Paisley gazed at the majesty of the Earth. No

other planet or moon could possibly compare to the wonderful planet they were lucky enough to call home. The thought of home made her heart ache. "I miss Dad. I miss Mom. I miss my bed."

"I miss mint chocolate chip ice cream," Ben said.

"I miss my basement laboratory."

"I miss our friends. Right now, I even miss Whitney-Raelynn."

Paisley grinned. "And I miss Newton." Newton. Newton! That's it! Paisley could almost see the light bulb flashing above her head. "Newton's Three Laws of Motion!"

"What?"

She jumped up and rummaged around in the Space Flyer as she talked. "We don't need fuel for the whole trip. Newton's first law. An object in motion will stay in motion. If we can just launch ourselves far enough to escape the moon's gravitational pull, then we'll continue in motion until we hit Earth's gravitational pull, which will be strong enough to bring us home."

"That would work, except we don't have even a

drop of fuel left," Ben said.

"Newton's third law. For every action, there is an opposite and equal reaction. We just need to create an action where the reaction will send us in the opposite direction, hurtling off into space."

"In theory, yes, but how—"

"With this!" Paisley held up the bungee cord they'd used to tie the fuel canister to the wagon. "We'll make a slingshot. We use force to pull back on the stretchy cord. When we release the pressure, the Space Flyer's reaction will be to launch forward, hopefully into space!"

Ben nodded. "Brilliant!"

They worked quickly. They looped the bungee cord around the rock outcropping they'd just been sitting on. Then they backed up behind the rock, stretching the bungee as far as it could possibly stretch. Holding the cord taut, they looped it around the wagon. Ben did his calculations in his head, and they aimed the Space Flyer for home.

"Ready? One, two, three!" Paisley chanted. They

leaped into their seats and released the slingshot.

Whoosh! They hurtled into space.

CHAPTER SEVEN
HOME SWEET HOME

The trip back to Earth was slightly terrifying. The Space Flyer plunged through the Earth's atmosphere at a speed so swift, the compressed air around them caught fire. The ship's wooden wings darkened and the couch cushions sizzled. Paisley and Ben could feel the heat of the flames licking at their coats.

And then they were through the atmosphere and spinning toward the Earth's surface. Ben let loose the sheet they'd packed like a parachute. The Space Flyer floated right into Paisley's backyard.

"Wow," Paisley said. The poor wagon was scorched almost black.

"Let's not do that again for awhile," Ben said.

"Deal," Paisley agreed. They removed their still-

smoking space gear and lugged the two couch cushions back into the house.

Dad was cooking in the kitchen. "Hi, guys! What's that smell?"

"Atmosphere," Paisley said with a giggle. Newton scampered up her leg and curled himself around her neck.

Dad came into the living room, wiping his hands on his pants. "What happened to the couch cushions?"

Paisley and Ben looked at the couch. Two of the couch cushions were stained with red dust, ripped in several places, and the corners were slightly charred. "The collateral damage of scientific exploration and investigation?" Paisley said in her sweetest voice.

Dad just laughed. "Did you find any aliens?"

Paisley grinned. "We found something even better. Home."

"I can't wait to hear all about it," Dad said. "Come eat my chicken enchiladas and Mexican rice, and tell me everything. We'll get Mom up on Skype. Ben, you have time for supper, don't you?"

"Yes, sir!" Ben said.

Paisley followed them into the kitchen. She scratched Newton's fur. Then she frowned. Everything had turned out fine. So why did she still feel like she was forgetting something important?

Over at the Pendlebury's scrubbed and spotless home, Mrs. Pendlebury entered the bathroom without her glasses. Her vision blurry, she glimpsed the full bathtub. Her husband must have drawn it for her, in appreciation for how hard she worked to maintain an orderly household, Mrs. Pendlebury thought.

She slipped into the bath and closed her eyes,

enjoying the peace and quiet. She was completely relaxed. Suddenly, Mrs. Pendlebury felt something very strange. Something was nibbling on her toes!

Her ear-piercing shriek could be heard throughout the entire neighborhood.

Science Alliance!
Build Your Own Telescope Materials

Materials:
- two lenses with different focal lengths (such as 150 mm and 500 mm double convex lenses. An adult can order them on Amazon.com)
- paper towel roll
- one piece of cardstock
- tape

Step 1
Roll the cardstock the long way to form a tube that is the diameter of the lens with the shortest focal length. This lens is the eyepiece. Tape the tube.

Step 2
Tape the edges of the eyepiece lens to one end of the paper tube.

Step 3

Tape the second lens to the end of the paper towel roll. Put the free end of the paper tube into the cardboard tube.

Step 4

Use your telescope! Look through the eyepiece, pointing the other end of the telescope at a distant object. Slide the two tubes in and out until the object focuses. If it isn't focusing, try a longer tube like a wrapping paper roll. The image will be upside down. It will be magnified, so the object will appear larger than it is. Scientists use telescopes to see distant planets, moons, and stars in space!

Women in Science

Dr. Sally Ride was the first American woman and the youngest American astronaut in space. She flew two space missions. She founded NASA's Office of Exploration and wrote seven books on space for kids. She created Sally Ride Science, a program focused on creating engaging science and engineering programs for girls.

Sally Ride (1951–2012)

Author Q & A

Q. **What did you enjoy most about writing** *Spacing Out?*

A. I loved all the cool facts I learned about outer space in my research.

Q. **What planet or moon would you visit if you could?**

A. I would definitely want to check out Titan. I want to hang glide like Paisley did with her jacket!

Q. **Do you believe in aliens?**

A. I am not sure if there are other beings out there as intelligent as humans. And I doubt they would look like little green men. But I think there are probably life forms of some sort on other planets, maybe in galaxies far beyond the Milky Way.

Silly Science!

What kind of music do planets sing?

Neptunes!

How do you know when the moon has had enough to eat?

When it's full!

How does the solar system hold up its pants?

With an asteroid belt!

Websites to Visit

Learn about outer space:

http://amazingspace.org

Join NASA's kids club!

www.nasa.gov/audience/forkids/kidsclub/flash/
 index.html#.VsYZ0fkrLWI

Learn about astronomy:

www.kidsastronomy.com

About the Author

Kyla Steinkraus lives with her husband, two kids, and two spoiled cats in Atlanta, Georgia. She loves writing about strong female characters like Paisley Atoms. Her favorite things about space are the gorgeous images of stars from the Hubble Space Telescope. In her free time, Kyla loves reading, photography, hiking, traveling, and playing games with her family.

About the Illustrator

Alan Brown's love of comic art, cartoons and drawing has driven him to follow his dreams of becoming an artist. His career as a freelance artist and designer has allowed him to work on a wide range of projects, from magazine illustration and game design to children's books. He's had the good fortune to work on comics such as *Ben 10* and *Bravest Warriors*. Alan lives in Newcastle with his wife, sons and dog.